First published by Parragon in 2013
Parragon
Chartist House
15–17 Trim Street
Bath BA1 1HA, UK
www.parragon.com

Written by David Bedford
Illustrated by Brenna Vaughan and Henry St Leger
Edited by Laura Baker
Designed by Ailsa Cullen
Production by Rob Simenton

ISBN 978-1-4723-0292-2

Printed in China

I love my Grandma

PaRragon

Bath · New York · Singapore · Hong Kong · Cologne · Delhi
Melbourne · Amsterdam · Johannesburg · Shenzhen

Little Hedgehog and Grandma Hedgehog
loved to play hide-and-seek together.
One day, when Grandma went to find
Little Hedgehog...

Little Hedgehog hid! He put
his paws over his mouth so
that Grandma couldn't hear
him giggling.

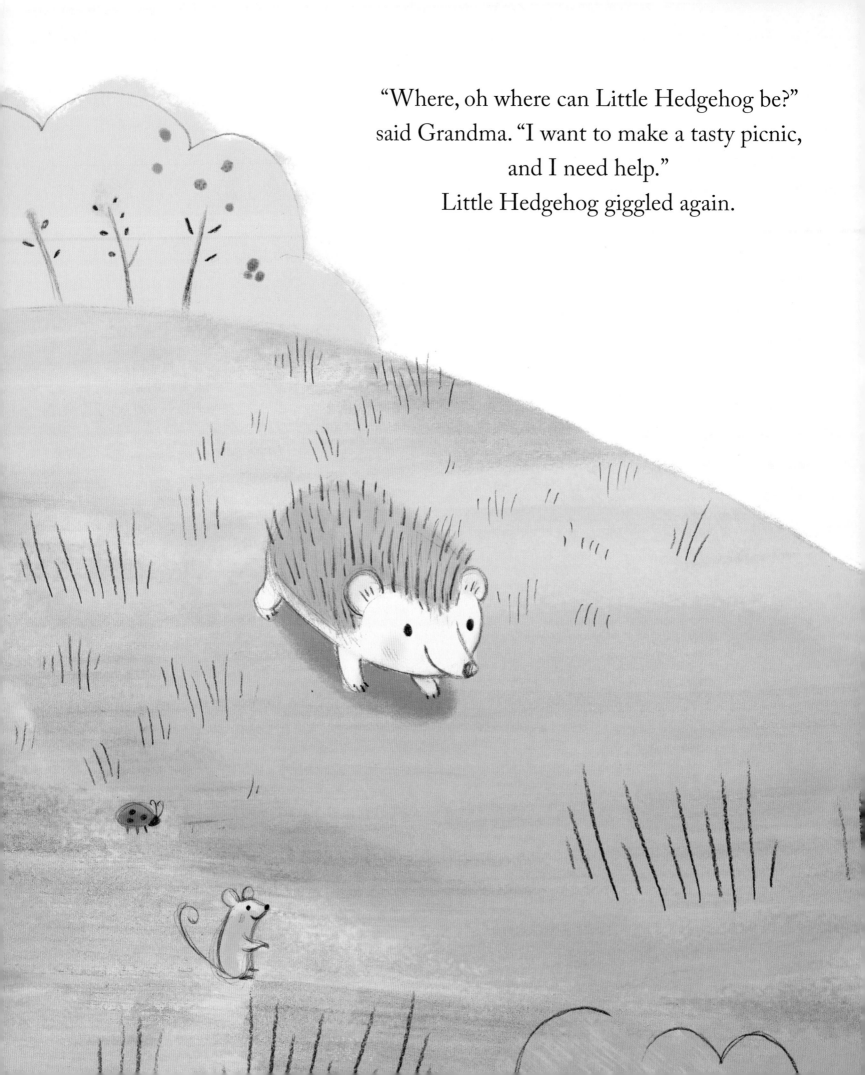

"Where, oh where can Little Hedgehog be?"
said Grandma. "I want to make a tasty picnic,
and I need help."
Little Hedgehog giggled again.

"Oh, well," said Grandma. "I shall have
to make the picnic myself."
Little Hedgehog followed closely
behind Grandma.

"I wish Little Hedgehog were here to help me pick juicy blackberries," said Grandma.

When she wasn't looking, Little Hedgehog picked the **biggest blackberries** he could reach… and put them into Grandma's basket!

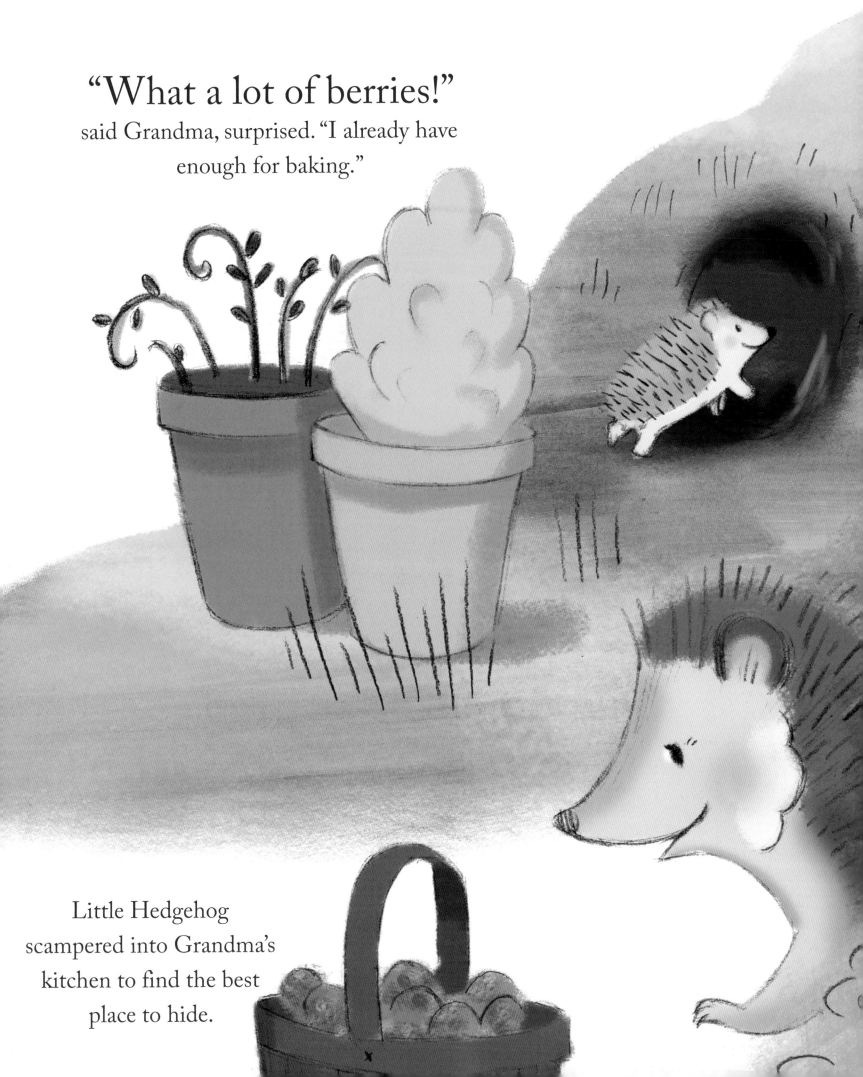

"What a lot of berries!"
said Grandma, surprised. "I already have
enough for baking."

Little Hedgehog
scampered into Grandma's
kitchen to find the best
place to hide.

Little Hedgehog crouched down low
so that Grandma couldn't see him.

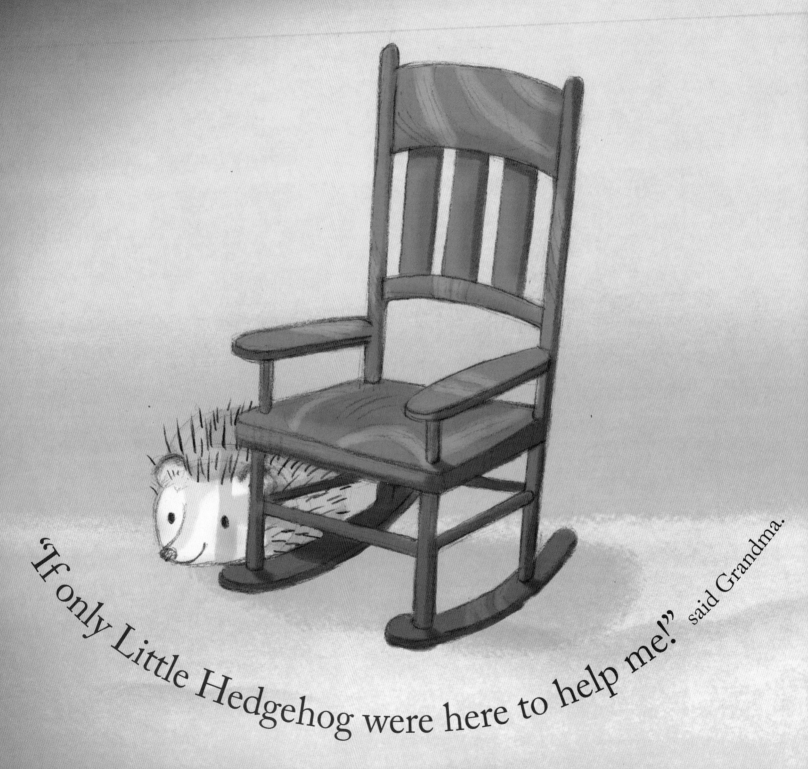

"If only Little Hedgehog were here to help me!" said Grandma.

Little Hedgehog giggled again. Then he licked his lips as Grandma
Hedgehog poured sweet, scrumptious honey into her mixing bowl.

"Honey is my treat for Little Hedgehog," said Grandma.
Little Hedgehog crept out from his hiding place…

He tried not to make a sound as he tasted the honey for himself, but it was too tasty!

"Yum!"
whispered Little Hedgehog.

Then he hurried back to his hiding place. Suddenly...

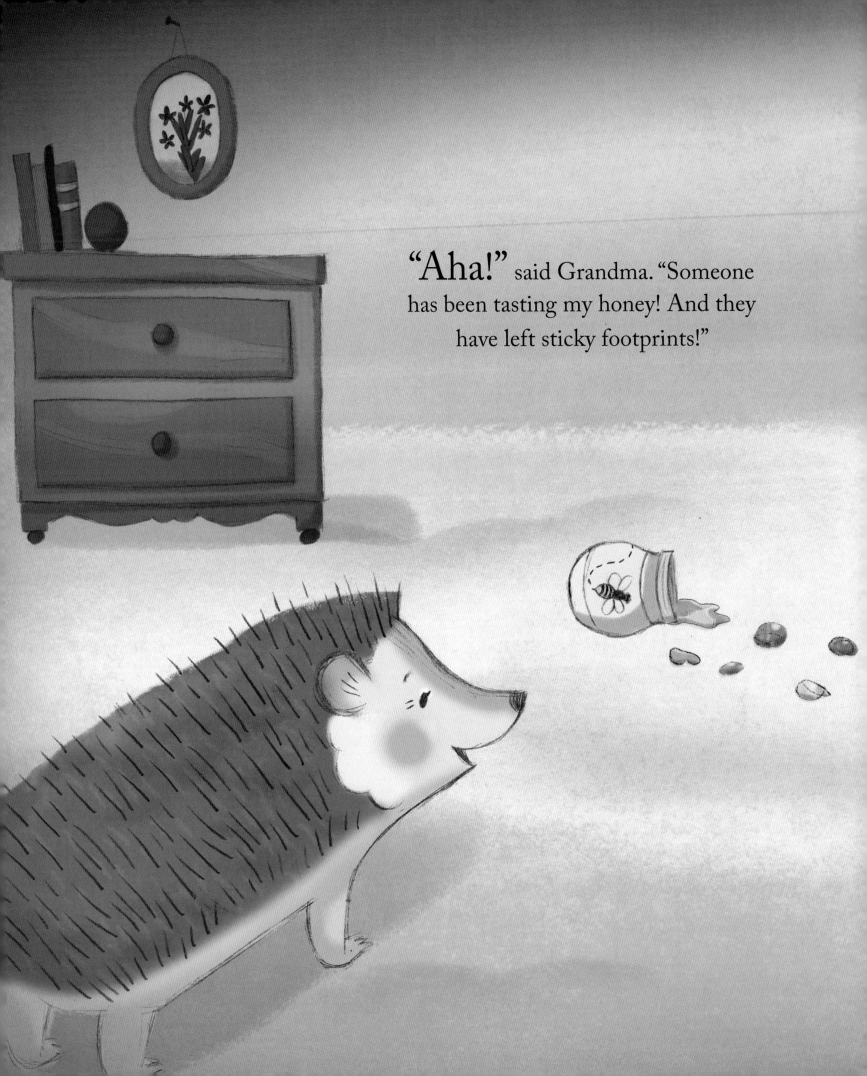

"Aha!" said Grandma. "Someone has been tasting my honey! And they have left sticky footprints!"

"Oh, no!" Little Hedgehog didn't want to be found. Not yet!

Grandma followed the

teeny,

tiny,

sticky

footprints

across the kitchen.

"Someone has been playing hide-and-seek
with me!" she said, smiling. Then…

"I've found you, Little Hedgehog!" said Grandma.

But Little Hedgehog
wasn't behind the
rocking chair.

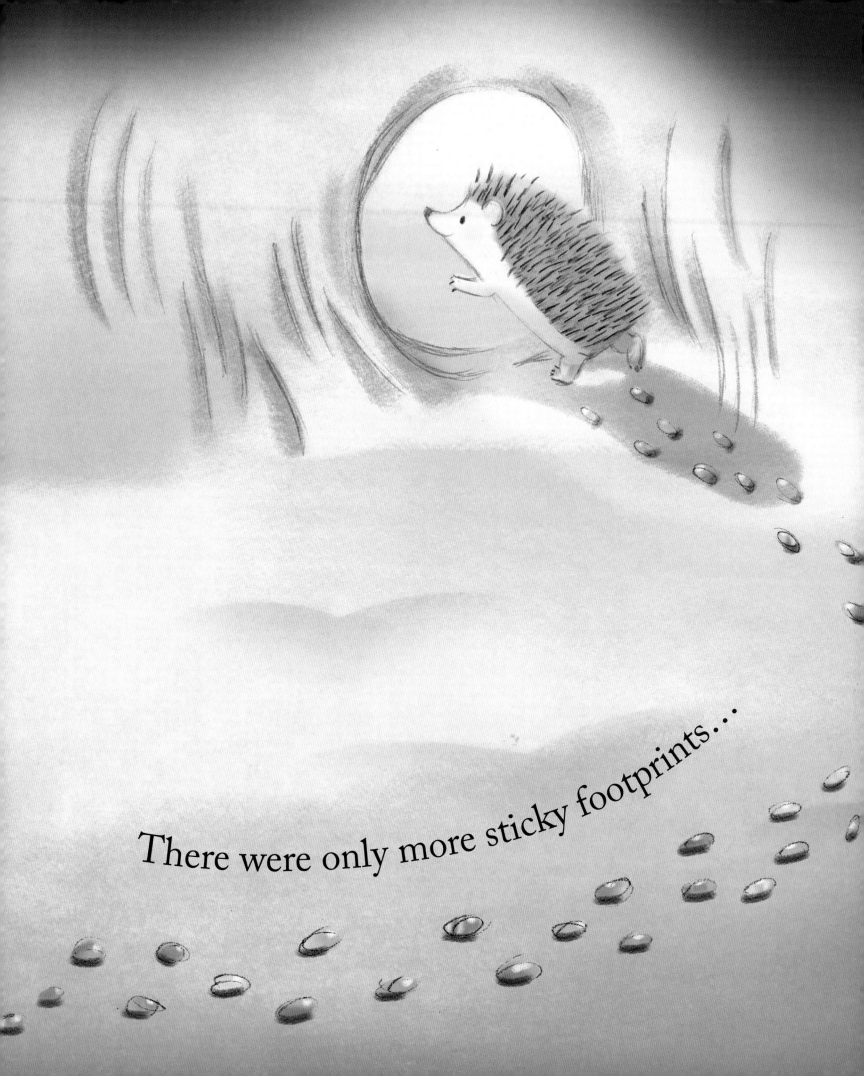

There were only more sticky footprints...

Grandma followed the sticky footprints out of
the kitchen and into the garden.

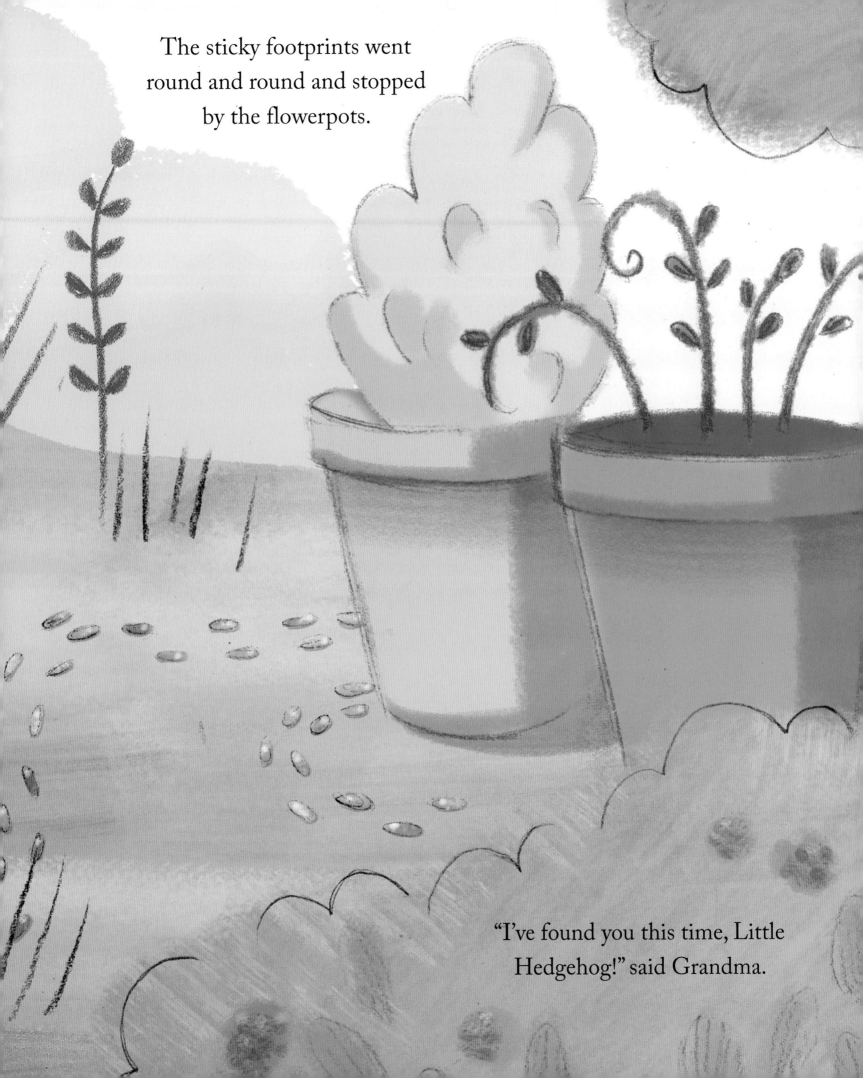

The sticky footprints went round and round and stopped by the flowerpots.

"I've found you this time, Little Hedgehog!" said Grandma.

But Little Hedgehog wasn't behind the flowerpots! He was… inside one!

"Surprise!"
said Little Hedgehog, giggling as he gave Grandma a big hug.

"Well done, Little Hedgehog," said his grandma. "You are the best at hide-and-seek. And I hope you are hungry, because our picnic is ready!"

"I am hungry!" said Little Hedgehog. But when he looked around the garden, he couldn't see a picnic anywhere. "Where is it?" he asked. Grandma giggled.

"You have to find it!" she said.

Little Hedgehog searched
around the garden and
soon found…

honey cookies…

and fruit salad.

Then Grandma brought out a
giant blackberry and honey cake.

"Yum!"

said Little Hedgehog.
It was the best he had ever tasted.

"I love Grandma's picnics!"
Little Hedgehog shouted happily. "And…

"I love my grandma!"